WOLVERINE
and
LITTLE THUNDER

An Eel Fishing Story

ALAN SYLIBOY

NIMBUS
PUBLISHING LTD.
— NIMBUS.CA —

Nimbus Publishing Limited
3660 Strawberry Hill Street, Halifax, NS, B3K 5A5
(902) 455-4286 nimbus.ca

NB1437

Printed and bound in Canada

Editor: Whitney Moran
Design: Jenn Embree

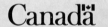 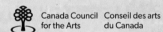 

Library and Archives Canada Cataloguing in Publication

Title: Wolverine and Little Thunder : an eel fishing story / Alan Syliboy.
Names: Syliboy, Alan, author, illustrator.
Description: "Bestselling author of The thundermaker."
Identifiers: Canadiana (print) 20189068752 | Canadiana (ebook) 20189068760 | ISBN 9781771087278 (hardcover) | ISBN 9781771087285 (HTML)
Classification: LCC PS8637.Y39 W65 2019 | DDC jC813/.6—dc23

Nimbus Publishing acknowledges the financial support for its publishing activities from the Government of Canada through the Canada Book Fund (CBF) and the Canada Council for the Arts, and from the Province of Nova Scotia. We are pleased to work in partnership with the Province of Nova Scotia to develop and promote our creative industries for the benefit of all Nova Scotians.

Little Thunder's home was far away from other people. He lived alone with his father and mother, and he had no playmates.

But he had a great many animal friends,
and his favourite of all was Wolverine.

Now, Wolverine was a super athlete.

He could jump from treetop to treetop and travel long distances without touching the ground.

He was also a great swimmer, and could hold his breath longer than anyone.

Wolverine was impossible to beat in a fight. Even when he was beaten and dismembered, he could reassemble himself and win the fight. Once Wolverine discovered he was indestructible, it made him all the more daring, and often reckless.

As we will see, this would complicate Little Thunder's life.

Wolverine was famous for being strong and fierce and loyal and helpful, but he was also known for being a trickster. That's why the Elders of the community respected him so much, and they taught Little Thunder to respect Wolverine as well.

Even though Little Thunder and Wolverine were very different, they became friends quickly.

Little Thunder lived in a wigwam with his parents.
It was a very orderly and comfortable home.

Wolverine lived in a hole dug under a tree. His home was comfortable, but not very orderly.

But Wolverine and Little Thunder had one important thing in common: Little Thunder was being groomed to take his father's place as the Thundermaker, and Wolverine was preparing to assist his friend in this role when the time came.

Early in the morning, Wolverine would meet Little Thunder at his wigwam, and the two would go in search of the caribou herd that was usually nearby. They became better and better at guessing where the herd had moved since they last saw it.

Once they found the herd, they'd observe the caribou as they grazed on the long grasses, watching to see if a new calf had been born.

Working as a team, Wolverine and Little Thunder would sneak up on their prey.

Little Thunder would get the herd to move in Wolverine's direction, but Wolverine, being impulsive, would pounce too early, and the attack would fail.

Though they enjoyed hunting caribou, their favourite pastime was eel fishing. They fished in the summer and they fished in the winter. Eel fishing was fun, and eel meat was their favourite meat of all.

In the winter, they would get a stone axe and cut through the ice. Using a very long spear, they would poke around in the mud until they speared an eel.

In the summer, they used a canoe, and fished all night with a torch. They would also catch eels in the fish weirs with stones on the river, and would funnel the eels into a basket.

But Wolverine and Little Thunder loved
to spear eels best of all.

One summer night, when the moon was full, they lit a torch and went out on the river. Everything was going well. They had caught a couple of eels, and Wolverine was at the front of the boat, taking a turn with the spear.

Little Thunder's mind wandered. He remembered the stories his father had told him about a giant eel that lived in this river…

An eel that was too big to catch.
An eel that could turn the tables on whoever hunted it.

As Wolverine was poking around in the mud,
he felt something stir. He'd woken the great eel!

It rose out of the water, all one hundred feet of it, with strength to match its size.

The eel pulled Wolverine overboard. The fight was on. Little Thunder watched in fear from the back of the boat.

As Wolverine was pulled underwater, he thought about how the giant eel could provide enough meat to get his community through the coming winter.

They landed on the lake bottom. Wolverine was an excellent diver, but now he was in a fight for his life. The eel coiled around Wolverine, keeping him from the surface, trying to drown him.

With his death-grip, the eel could defeat any opponent, but Wolverine was immortal. As the two fought, the water churned and it sounded to Little Thunder as if a tornado were trying to suck up the river.

Little Thunder watched this contest amazed. The moonlight on the water giving it a strange beauty. Little Thunder was very worried about his friend and thought there was no way Wolverine could defeat the eel in his own backyard.

Then suddenly…the river became quiet.

Wolverine poked his head out of the water. "Give me your rope," he said to Little Thunder. "We will pull the eel to shore."

They pulled at the rope,
but the eel did not want
to come to shore.

They pulled and pulled with all their strength. They were almost ready to give up, when a moose happened by. Little Thunder asked for his help, and the moose was glad to assist.

The three pulled the eel's massive body all day long, and got it to shore just as the sun was starting to set. Wolverine chopped off the eel's head with the stone axe, and that was the end of him.

Little Thunder had cleaned eels for his mother, Giju, but this eel was beyond his experience, so he ran home to get her.

It took three days to skin and clean the giant eel, but Wolverine was right. There would be enough meat for the winter.

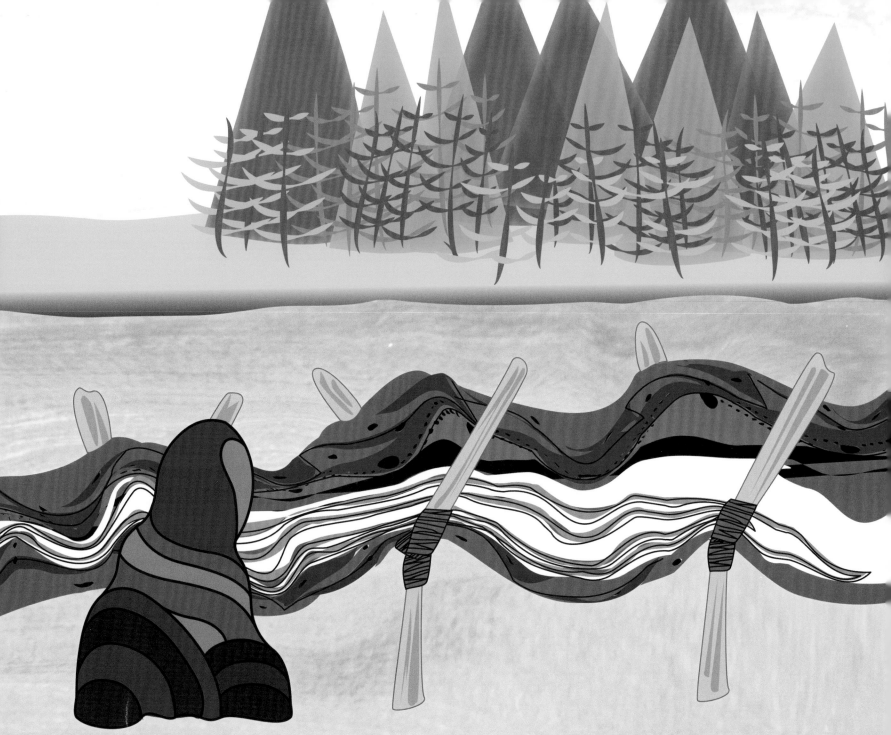

The eel skin was as long as a forest path. Wolverine and Little Thunder were determined that no part of the animal be wasted. After letting the skin dry in the sun for three more days...

They made a canoe out of it.